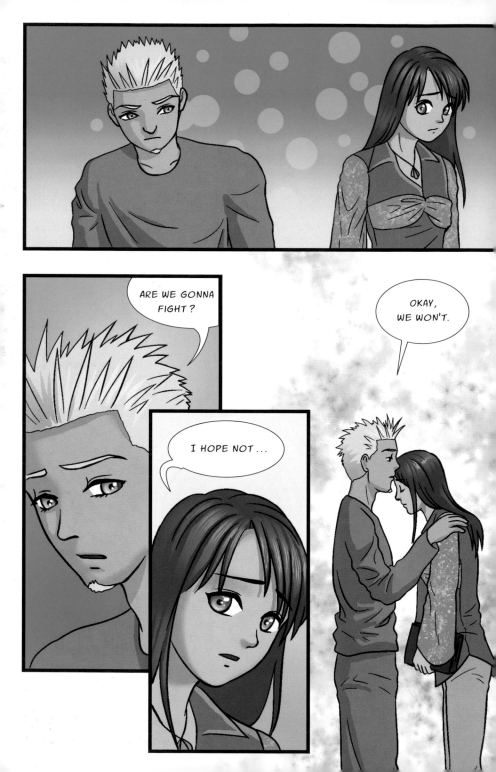

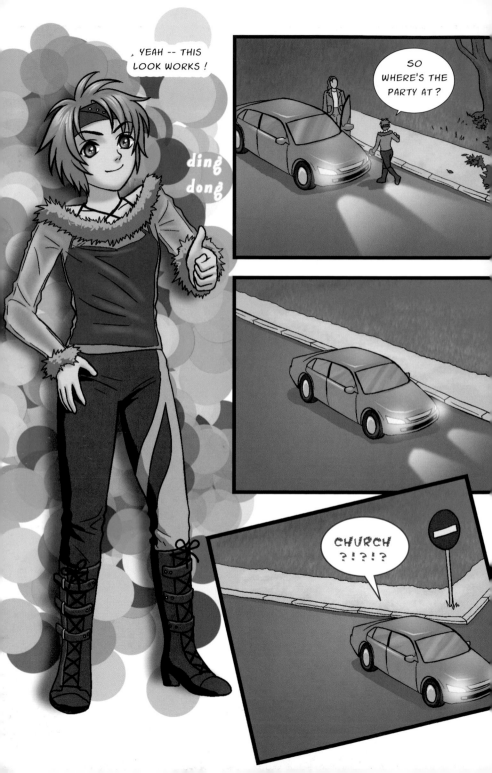

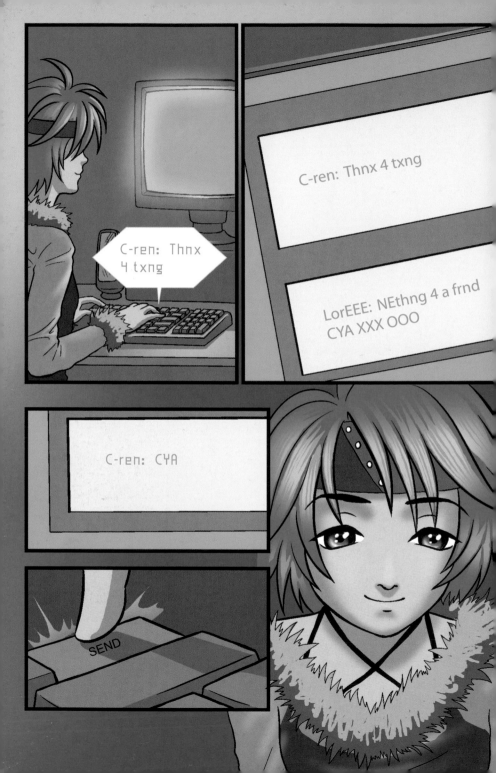

* Methamphetamine

* See "Bad Girl in Tow

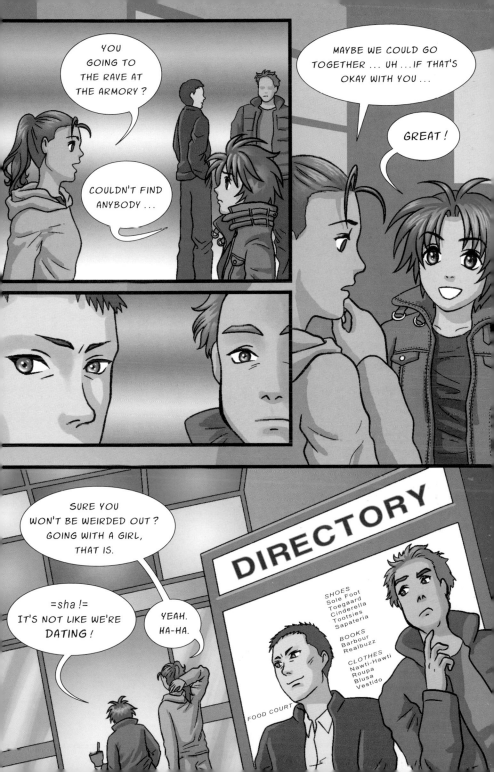

STILL, HOW CAN WE HELP HER IF WE DON'T SHARE GOOD THINGS?
BUT IF I WANNA SEE DEREK I GOTTA PUT UP WITH KIMBERLY!
THUMPAWHUMPAW
WELL, SHE'S NOT GOING TO SPOIL MY FUN! I'LL JUST IGNORE HER!

Serenity – VERSION 1

REALBUZZ STUDIOS ORIGINALLY CONCEIVED Serenity AS A FULL COLOR
MONTHLY COMICS MAGAZINE. CHANGES IN THE MAGAZINE INDUSTRY MADE
LAUNCHING Serenity DIFFICULT; MATTERS WERE FURTHER COMPLICATED
WHEN A SCHEDULING CONFLICT DEPRIVED US OF OUR ORIGINAL ARTIST.
REPACKAGED AS A SERIES OF ORIGINAL MANGA GRAPHIC NOVELS, Serenity
ALMOST IMMEDIATELY ATTRACTED PUBLISHER INTEREST AND SOON WAS
SNATCHED UP BY BARBOUR PUBLISHING. FOR MORE FUN Serenity
FACTOIDS, BE SURE TO VISIT WWW.SERENITYBUZZ.COM AND
WWW.REALBUZZSTUDIOS.COM.

Chapter

THERE'S A REASON AND A PURPOSE BEHIND EVERYTHING THE PRAYER CLUB DOES!
HERE'S WHERE THEY FIND GUIDANCE AND MEANING FOR THEIR LIVES :

"HOW LONG MUST I WRESTLE WITH
MY THOUGHTS AND EVERY DAY HAVE
SORROW IN MY HEART?"

Psalm 13:2
(New International Version)

"NOW FAITH IS BEING SURE OF WHAT WE
HOPE FOR AND CERTAIN OF WHAT WE
DO NOT SEE....BY FAITH WE UNDER-
STAND THAT THE UNIVERSE WAS FORMED
AT GOD'S COMMAND...."

Hebrews 11: 1, 3 (NIV)

"'FOR I KNOW THE PLANS I
HAVE FOR YOU,' DECLARES
THE LORD, 'PLANS TO PROS-
PER YOU AND NOT TO HARM
YOU, PLANS TO GIVE YOU
HOPE AND A FUTURE.'"

Jeremiah 29:11 (NIV)

and ♡Verse

"FOR THEY MOUTH EMPTY, BOASTFUL WORDS AND, BY APPEALING TO THE LUSTFUL DESIRES OF SINFUL HUMAN NATURE, THEY ENTICE PEOPLE WHO ARE JUST ESCAPING FROM THOSE WHO LIVE IN ERROR."

2 Peter 2:18 (NIV)

"SUBMIT YOURSELVES, THEN, TO GOD. RESIST THE DEVIL, AND HE WILL FLEE FROM YOU."

James 4:7 (NIV)

"JESUS LOOKED AT THEM AND SAID, 'WITH MAN THIS IS IMPOSSIBLE, BUT NOT WITH GOD; ALL THINGS ARE POSSIBLE WITH GOD.'"

Mark 10:27 (NIV)

BOTTOM LINE:
"AS A SHEPHERD LOOKS AFTER HIS SCATTERED FLOCK WHEN HE IS WITH THEM, SO WILL I LOOK AFTER MY SHEEP. I WILL RESCUE THEM FROM ALL THE PLACES WHERE THEY WERE SCATTERED ON A DAY OF CLOUDS AND DARKNESS."

Ezekiel 34:12 (NIV)

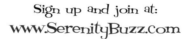

Watch for more of
SERENITY'S STORY!

Serenity slides closer to Derek.

Ah, the painful lesson she'll learn. . . .

Volume 5
Snow Biz
Is Available July 2006

Serenity views a Prayer Club ski trip as one more opportunity to drive a wedge between Derek and Kimberly. But while hot-dogging on the slopes, Serenity takes a major tumble, breaking her leg and seriously bruising her ego. Who's going to care for Serenity's wounds—both physical and spiritual?

future title:

You Shall Love—Available September 2006

Serenity

ART BY MIN KWON
CREATED BY BUZZ DIXON
ORIGINAL CHARACTER DESIGNS
BY DRIGZ ABROT

SERENITY THROWS A BIG WET SLOPPY ONE OUT TO:
MICHELLE C., NOAH S., JASON P., RANDY M., AND JOMAR B.

LUV U GUYZ !!!

©&TM 2006 by Realbuzz Studios   ISBN 1-59310-873-7

Published by Barbour Publishing, Inc., P.O. Box 719, Uhrichsville, Ohio 44683
www.barbourbooks.com

"OUR MISSION IS TO PUBLISH AND DISTRIBUTE
INSPIRATIONAL PRODUCTS OFFERING EXCEPTIONAL VALUE
AND BIBLICAL ENCOURAGEMENT TO THE MASSES."

ecpa Member of the
Evangelical Christian
Publishers Association

Scripture quotations marked NIV are taken from
The HOLY BIBLE, NEW INTERNATIONAL VERSION®. NIV®.
Copyright © 1973, 1978, 1984 by International Bible Society.
Used by permission of Zondervan. All rights reserved.

Printed in China.
5 4 3 2 1

VISIT **SERENITY** AT:
www.Serenitybuzz.com
www.RealbuzzStudios.com